Aphrodisiac

by Rob Handel

SAMUEL FRENCH

FOUNDED 1830

NEW YORK HOLLYWOOD LONDON TORONTO

SAMUELFRENCH.COM

ISBN 978-0-573-69890-3   Printed in U.S.A.   #29682

MUSIC USE NOTE

Licensees are solely responsible for obtaining formal written permission from copyright owners to use copyrighted music in the performance of this play and are strongly cautioned to do so. If no such permission is obtained by the licensee, then the licensee must use only original music that the licensee owns and controls. Licensees are solely responsible and liable for all music clearances and shall indemnify the copyright owners of the play and their licensing agent, Samuel French, Inc., against any costs, expenses, losses and liabilities arising from the use of music by licensees.

IMPORTANT BILLING AND CREDIT REQUIREMENTS

All producers of *APHRODISIAC* *must* give credit to the Author of the Play in all programs distributed in connection with performances of the Play, and in all instances in which the title of the Play appears for the purposes of advertising, publicizing or otherwise exploiting the Play and/or a production. The name of the Author *must* appear on a separate line on which no other name appears, immediately following the title and *must* appear in size of type not less than fifty percent of the size of the title type.

In addition the following credit *must* be given in all programs and publicity information distributed in association with this piece:

Originally produced in New York City by 13P, January 2005

Subsequently produced by Long Wharf Theatre, December 7, 2005 (Gordon Edelstein, Artistic Director; Michael Stotts, Managing Director)

APHRODISIAC was originally produced in New York City by 13P on January 7, 2005. It was directed by Ken Rus Schmoll, with sets by Sue Rees, costumes by Michelle R. Phillips, lighting by Garin Marschall, and sound by Bray Poor. The production stage managers were Carrie Meconis and Rebecca Spinac. The cast was as follows:

ALMA..Jennifer Dundas
AVERY..Thomas Jay Ryan
MONICA ....Alison Weller

APHRODISIAC was subsequently produced by Long Wharf Theatre on December 7, 2005 (Gordon Edelstein, Artistic Director; Michael Stotts, Managing Director). It was directed by Ken Rus Schmoll, with sets by Sue Rees, costumes by Michelle R. Phillips, lighting by Garin Marschall, sound by Bray Poor, and dramaturgy by Beatrice Basso. The production stage manager was Charles M. Turner III. The cast was as follows:

ALMA..Jennifer Dundas
AVERY...Rob Campbell
MONICA ....Yetta Gottesman

CHARACTERS

ALMA

AVERY

MONICA

SETTING

Washington, D.C. and New York City,
early summer 2001 and early summer 2002.

NOTE ON NAMES

The second syllable of "Ilona" is pronounced with a long o, as in "own" or "loan." The first syllable of "Alma" is pronounced "all."

WASHINGTON, D.C.

(A Korean restaurant. A man and a woman sit in a booth. **ALMA** *is 24 and looks her age.* **AVERY** *is 33 but stress has aged him badly.)*

ALMA. It's not that it's not fair, technically it IS fair, I was supposed to have a six-month internship, until I got my degree, but it's not like they weren't happy to have me working for free after that, but now with this, it's like they don't care how it looks on my résumé, they don't care that it looks irregular, like I was doing something irregular, and I would still be there, I would still be there working for free if I hadn't mentioned something in casual conversation about my graduation in December, that's what's not fair, I would still be there if it were not for pure chance, that's what's not fair.

AVERY. You want me to call her again?

ALMA. No, no. I understand it puts her in a funny position. I want to be there, but she doesn't want to look like she's taking advantage of me. Everything is always about appearances.

(pause)

I'm just thrown for a loop.

AVERY. Of course you are.

ALMA. It's just like, all these things, boom.

AVERY. Right.

ALMA. And I haven't been able to get a hold of you.

AVERY. I told you, my wife is flying in tomorrow.

ALMA. I thought she was too sick to travel.

AVERY. It's the first time in I don't know how many years. She really wanted to go to that dinner this year. They're giving some award to someone.

ALMA. Jessye Norman?

AVERY. Is he the guy who was a hostage in Iran? Anyway, I guess she wants to stay for a few weeks.

(pause)

Sorry it's a bad time. Is there anyone you want me to call?

ALMA. Like who?

AVERY. I don't know. Another internship? Maybe a job?

ALMA. With who?

AVERY. I don't know. What do you want to do?

ALMA. I want to be a senator.

AVERY. OK, but I meant have you thought about your immediate plans?

ALMA. I've given them some thought, yes.

AVERY. Is it anything I can help you with?

(ALMA looks at him a moment, and then begins to laugh.)

What?

(Her laughter goes on and on.)

What's so funny?

(He's been trying to share the joke, but now he becomes concerned: people are looking at them.)

Could you stop already?

(She is laughing and wiping her eyes.)

Ilona, come on.

(She stops and catches her breath. She wipes her eyes.)

ALMA. I'm pregnant and I've decided to move to New York and have the baby and wait.

AVERY. What do you mean wait?

ALMA. I'm just going to wait. I'll go to museums. New York is a good place to wait. You can drink coffee – if you're pregnant you can drink herbal tea – and watch the world go by. Very fast.

AVERY. That's ridiculous.

ALMA. Fuck you.

AVERY. Hey!

ALMA. You called me ridiculous.

AVERY. I said you're BEING ridiculous. I meant you're BEING ridiculous.

ALMA. Fuck you.

AVERY. Will you stop saying that.

ALMA. You used to like when I –

AVERY. Now STOP. What's gotten into you?

(She begins to laugh again.)

OK, I get that.

(She calms down.)

I'm trying to say, listen to yourself. Watching the world go by? You're young. You're full of life.

ALMA. You're pretty lively yourself.

AVERY. Will you listen?

ALMA. This is much more fun than I imagined.

AVERY. You can't put a stop on your life. You can't call everything off, you can't let this – this – random – fluke – of luck –

ALMA. Careful.

AVERY. *(continuous)* determine how you're going to spend the next 18 years of your life.

ALMA. How are you going to spend the next 18 years of YOUR life?

AVERY. *(continuous)* Are you thinking about that? Listen to me. You have an amazing life ahead of you. You're smart.

ALMA. Oh, thank you.

AVERY. *(continuous)* You're one of the smartest young people I've ever met.

ALMA. Funny how my age is suddenly a big subject.

AVERY. *(continuous)* You could be anything you want in this town. You don't want to leave Washington.

ALMA. Would you miss me?

AVERY. I'm thinking about you.

ALMA. Would you miss me?

AVERY. This is going to determine your whole future.

ALMA. Would you miss me?

AVERY. That's not something to throw away out of petulance.

ALMA. Would you miss me?

(pause)

But enough about me. How have you been?

AVERY. I care about you.

ALMA. You CARE about me? Like a parakeet?

AVERY. Let's talk about this in the car.

ALMA. Let's talk about it in bed.

AVERY. I think we need to focus –

ALMA. I'm not attractive to you anymore?

AVERY. Ilona. Give me a break here.

(AVERY checks his reflection in a piece of silverware. ALMA catches him. He rises, takes her arm.)

Come on.

(sees her amused expression)

What?

ALMA. You're afraid of me. It's really funny.

(She cracks up again.)

AVERY. Do you want to hurt me? Have I given you reason to hurt me?

(She doesn't budge. He tries a new tone.)

It must have been a great shock. Finding out you were pregnant. This is a confusing time for you.

ALMA. Not really.

AVERY. Let's go.

ALMA. I don't want to.

AVERY. Ilona –

ALMA. I don't want to. Why don't you sit down?

AVERY. We can't talk about this here.

ALMA. No one ever comes in this place. That's why you take me to eat here.

(**AVERY** *sits, takes a deep breath.*)

AVERY. Let's say you move to New York and have a kid. What do you think is going to happen?

ALMA. You'll come visit. After the kid is born.

AVERY. I can't do that.

ALMA. I'll sleep with you again if you do.

AVERY. That is the last thing on my mind right now.

(*Beat.* **ALMA** *explodes into uncontrolled laughter.*)

All right.

(*Her laughter continues.*)

Ha ha.

(*Her laughter continues.*)

We're going to get kicked out.

(*Her laughter continues.*)

It's not funny.

(*Her laughter winds down. Pause.*)

ALMA. The last thing on my mind.

(*She starts up again.*)

AVERY. Jesus God.

(**ALMA** *regains her composure. She smiles at* **AVERY.**)

ALMA. You'll come. I know you'll come.

AVERY. You're wrong, sweetie.

ALMA. We'll see.

AVERY. You're really overestimating yourself. You're thinking like a child.

(**ALMA** *begins to fill with a reckless anger.* **AVERY** *sees it happen and tries to undo his words.*)

AVERY. That's not like you.

ALMA. That's exactly like me. That's why you're here.

AVERY. What's that supposed to mean?

ALMA. You like children. Do you know how many times you told me you love my tight little cunt?

AVERY. *(rising, grabbing her arm)* Jesus, that's enough. –

ALMA. *(continuous)* Every time except twice. I know because that was what made me come. When you said that into my ear, I knew you were totally out of control.

AVERY. You've never seen me out of control.

(*He rises, firmly grasping her arm. She tries to yank it away, but he has too tight a grip. He pulls her to her feet and towards the door. She resists.*)

(*She tries to bite his hand. He snatches it away just in time, releasing her. She backs up to the table. They face off.*)

(*He moves towards her. She picks up a glass and throws it down on the floor, smashing it. He freezes. She picks up another glass and smashes it. He turns around, calmly, as if he was suddenly a mere passer-by, and walks out the door as she picks up all the plates and saucers and teacups and smashes them one by one.*)

(*The lights slowly fade. In the darkness we hear taped voices.*)

ALMA. *(ON TAPE)* Congressman Ferris, do you know what happened to Ilona Waxman?

AVERY. *(ON TAPE)* No, I do not.

ALMA. *(ON TAPE)* Did you have anything to do with her disappearance?

AVERY. *(ON TAPE)* No, I didn't.

ALMA. *(ON TAPE)* Did you say anything or do anything that could have caused her to drop out of sight?

AVERY. *(ON TAPE)* You know, Ilona and I never had a cross word.

(The lights gradually fade up on an apartment. It is so orderly you would think no one lives there. **AVERY** *sits brooding, drinking a bottle of beer. Tape continues.)*

ALMA. *(ON TAPE)* Do you have any idea if there was anyone who wanted to harm her?

AVERY. *(ON TAPE)* No.

ALMA. *(ON TAPE)* Did you cause anyone to harm her?

AVERY. *(ON TAPE)* No.

ALMA. *(ON TAPE)* Did you kill Ilona Waxman?

AVERY. *(ON TAPE)* I did not.

ALMA. *(ON TAPE)* Can you describe your relationship? What exactly was your relationship with Ilona Waxman?

(A key turns in the door and **ALMA** *enters.* **AVERY** *does not acknowledge her.* **ALMA** *drops her coat and bag on a chair. Tape continues.)*

AVERY. *(ON TAPE)* Well, I met Ilona last, uh, October. And um, we became very close. I met her in Washington, D.C.

ALMA. *(ON TAPE)* Very close, meaning…?

AVERY. *(ON TAPE)* We had a close relationship. I liked her very much.

ALMA. *(ON TAPE)* May I ask you, was it a sexual relation-ship?

AVERY. *(ON TAPE)* Well, Christine, I've been married for 34 years, and uh, I've not been a, a perfect man, and I've made my share of mistakes. But um, out of respect for my family, and out of a specific request from the Waxman family, I think it's best that I not get into those details, uh, about Ilona Waxman.

(Tape out. Silence. **ALMA** *gives up on waiting for* **AVERY** *to speak and picks up her coat as if to leave.)*

AVERY. *(suddenly)* What do you call that? I'll never be able to go in there again.

ALMA. Oh well.

(They speak in different voices than in the first scene – their own.)

AVERY. They had the best bibimbop in Virginia.

ALMA. You left me there. The cab ride cost me forty bucks.

(silence)

AVERY. Alma, this is getting out of hand.

ALMA. We've got to figure out what happened.

AVERY. Call me crazy, but I'm almost sure there are more traditional methods. Forensic evidence, that sort of thing.

ALMA. For God's sake, Avery. There are 558 open missing persons cases in Washington. I think it's safe to say the M.P.D.C. don't exactly specialize in locating –

AVERY. You don't know that. Something might turn up.

ALMA. Something might turn up in fifty years. Or never.

AVERY. Or tomorrow.

ALMA. And until then we're supposed to sit quietly and wait?

AVERY. It's better to break some poor restaurant's dishes?

ALMA. *(on "restaurant")* It's better for me, yes.

(pause)

AVERY. We could ask Dad. We could come right out and ask him what happened. We could say, Dad, we understand you're not ready to tell the whole world every detail of your personal life, but for us, within the family, we'd like you to tell us about –

ALMA. I'm not ready to speak to him. Besides, I know what he'll say.

AVERY. What?

ALMA. He'll deny everything.

AVERY. To us? To his children?

ALMA. What if I called him right now? Said I'm coming over? I get out of the cab. Smile at the doorman. Go up in the elevator. Ring the bell.

AVERY. *(in Dan's voice, rising)* Alma. Thanks for dropping by. How have you been?

ALMA. Are you going to offer me a drink, Dad?

AVERY. In fact I was.

ALMA. How civil.

AVERY. I know this is terrible for you and I'm sorry.

ALMA. *(on "and")* Bourbon and water.

AVERY. *(fixing drink)* No ice?

ALMA. Sorry I'm late. I was at my recovery group for children who have to picture a parent having sex because the whole world is doing so. Chelsea Clinton broke down again.

AVERY. When you're sarcastic you remind me of someone.

ALMA. Well, it's a Freudian nightmare all round.

(accepts drink, takes a swallow)

Were you having an affair with Ilona Waxman?

AVERY. *(immediately)* Yes.

ALMA. Jesus how pathetic.

(pause)

Don't you think?

(pause)

Do you miss her?

AVERY. My heart is broken.

ALMA. Is it. Did you ever love me?

AVERY. That's kind of a jump. Of subject.

ALMA. I'm suddenly curious.

AVERY. Yes, Alma, I love you very deeply.

ALMA. What's it been like?

AVERY. Like any father, I guess.

ALMA. *(on "I")* The past few days. How did you find out?

AVERY. Her mother called me. After they hadn't heard from her in five days.

ALMA. Did her mother know? About...

AVERY. No one knew. As far as I know, no one knew.

ALMA. How long had it been going on?

AVERY. Not long. A few months.

ALMA. Were you in – this is humiliating – Did you break up with her?

AVERY. No. We never fought. We never argued.

ALMA. Where did you think it would lead, for God's sake?

AVERY. Nowhere. I do this pretty often.

ALMA. Excuse me?

AVERY. I'm sorry. I do this pretty often. You can't be completely shocked, you know your mother and I –

ALMA. *(holding out her empty glass)* Could you?

AVERY. *(taking it)* – hardly ever see each other. You must have wondered.

ALMA. It's not something I thought about. Not being an intern myself, or a congressman, I actually think about things besides sex.

(He gives her the refreshed drink and resumes his story.)

AVERY. Her mother called. She asked me if I was having an affair with Ilona. I said no.

ALMA. You lied.

AVERY. It's nobody's business.

ALMA. She's missing. She could be dead.

AVERY. I feel terrible about that, but it's not because we were seeing each other. Probably something awful happened to her. It might be a random crime. It might have to do with some part of her life I didn't know about. But it's got nothing to do with me. There's no reason everyone has to know about us. You asked and I told you because you're my daughter.

ALMA. Bill Clinton lied to his daughter.

AVERY. I'm not Bill Clinton.

ALMA. That remains to be seen.

AVERY. After I hung up with her mother, I called a friend at the M.P.D.C. and told them to give the matter top priority. Then on Monday, the parents went to the Susan Burns Morgenstern Memorial Reward Foundation, which has a very effective public relations department, and within hours a 24-year-old adult working at the Bureau of Prisons became The Missing Intern and I became...

(vague gesture)

The reports started on the six o'clock news. I was in a subcommittee meeting that ran over. When I came out reporters started chasing me back to my office. I laid low with my staff for five hours. They wanted me to sneak out and stay with one of them, but I insisted on going to my own house. I had my personal cell phone turned off – the number I only give out to friends. I turned it on when I got home. Most of the messages were from women I've seen in the past ten years. The first one asked if I still had the book she gave me and asked me to throw it away. The second one asked if I still had the tie clip she gave me and asked me to throw it away. The third one – anyway, it went on from there.

(Sips his beer.)

The police questioned me for three hours yesterday. You probably know that, you probably saw Chief Showbiz on the news.

ALMA. Did you tell them the truth?

AVERY. No.

ALMA. For crying out loud, Dad!

AVERY. It's nobody's business. It's not going to help them find her.

ALMA. You didn't think Monica Lewinsky was nobody's business.

AVERY. I thought it was sordid. In the Oval Office!

ALMA. *(giving up)* Adultery is really its own moral universe.

AVERY. Ilona is an adult. I'm an adult. We were both lonely people and we enjoyed being together. I'm sorry she's missing and I'm angry that people are suggesting I might have had something to do with it. I'm angry that my life could be ruined. I'm angry that I'm being judged.

ALMA. That's three angries to one sorry.

(beat)

Was there a message from Mom?

AVERY. No.

ALMA. You're kidding. The house must be surrounded by reporters. She didn't call.

AVERY. Nope.

ALMA. Is that how you guys deal with these things? Silence? Pretense? Never mind, I don't want to know. No, I do. No, I don't. Mom must have called.

AVERY. I guess she was waiting for me to call her.

ALMA. Did you?

AVERY. I didn't have anything to say.

ALMA. *(a suggestion)* "I'm sorry I ruined your life."

AVERY. *(ignoring this)* I couldn't sleep, of course. I kept watching Headline News. It's interesting, actually. The way they repeat the same stories every half hour. Making little alterations in the order and phrasing even when they have no new information. A rumor becomes part of the story at 1:30, then disappears by 2:30. As if they have someone whose job is to make them up, to keep people awake. Finally I picked up the phone because I needed to talk to someone and, you know, your mother and I have been married for 34 years.

ALMA. She was probably thinking the same thing. How can I be there for him?

AVERY. I'll tell you one thing, Alma, she wasn't angry and sarcastic and thinking only of herself.

ALMA. No, thinking only of yourself is your job, isn't it?

AVERY. You'll excuse me, I have some work to do.

ALMA. What did Mom say?

AVERY. I don't care to share that with you right now. Where are you staying? I'll give you a ride on my hog.

(Pause. ALMA and AVERY crack up.)

AVERY. He SAYS that.

ALMA. I know, I know.

(They collapse, weeping with laughter. AVERY puts his hands out in front of him on imaginary handlebars.)

AVERY. Vroom, vroom!

(This sets them off again.)

ALMA. *(wiping her eyes)* Can you imagine him giving me a ride through the streets of Washington? Sitting behind him with my arms around his waist? I'd be on the cover of every paper. The new girlfriend.

AVERY. Jesus.

ALMA. *(barely able to speak)* I know, it makes me want to throw up.

(Their laughter subsides.)

AVERY. We've got to figure out what we're going to do.

ALMA. OK.

AVERY. Why don't you go see him?

ALMA. Why don't you go see him?

(Stalemate)

Have you talked to him at all?

AVERY. No.

ALMA. He didn't call?

AVERY. He never calls. I call him. Actually I don't call him, I call Mom, and she passes messages back and forth. You know, the clearinghouse.

ALMA. You and Dad live in the same city and you don't call? You don't have lunch?

AVERY. I bump into him. We get coffee.

ALMA. I'm hungry.

AVERY. Yeah, well, next time we go out, why don't you wait until they bring our food before you trash the place.

ALMA. Do you have any bread? I want to make toast.

AVERY. No.

ALMA. You don't have bread? How about a frozen bagel?

AVERY. Nope.

ALMA. What, you have nothing in your fridge except a jar of pickles, like Ilona Waxman? I hate Washington.

AVERY. As a representative of the mayor's office, I feel I should respond to that.

(pause)

The museums are nice.

(He gets another beer from the fridge.)

What's the worst-case scenario? He's hiding something terrible. He's done something we never thought he was capable of. Truthfully, I wouldn't have thought he was capable of having an affair. I would have thought he was too averse to risk.

ALMA. Like Bill Clinton?

AVERY. Maybe Dad didn't see it as a risk. Maybe he saw it as part of the job. He's a consummate professional.

ALMA. Like Bill Clinton.

AVERY. Best-case scenario. Benefit of the doubt. It was an innocent friendship. Here's this young woman. She and her friend – what's the friend's name?

ALMA. Trish.

AVERY. She and Trish are grad students in public administration. They go on what they call "political field trips" where they visit the offices of House members and have their photo taken with them. One day, they visit the representative from Ilona's home town. Trish talks herself into an internship in the office, but Ilona, Ilona's already interning at the Bureau of Prisons. But she and Dad get to be friends. They call each other often. Maybe there's an element of flirtation, maybe not. Then she disappears. He is questioned. He tries, perhaps misguidedly, to protect her reputation, and as a result he is crucified in the media. Anything could have happened to that girl. She could have let herself get picked up by a serial killer in a bar. She went jogging alone at night. This is not a bright girl.

ALMA. You don't know that. She was an independent adult.

AVERY. She was having an affair with a married womanizer congressman.

ALMA. Have you never been involved in a stupid doomed self-destructive affair? Love, sex, whatever, makes you do stupid things. That doesn't mean you're stupid. That doesn't mean you routinely put your life in danger.

AVERY. May I answer the question? No, I've never been involved in a stupid affair.

ALMA. Have you ever been involved in a smart affair?

AVERY. Well, Alma, I've not been a perfect man.

ALMA. Funny.

(Pause. AVERY sips his beer.)

AVERY. One thing you can say: now everyone in the 18th District knows who their congressman is.

ALMA. Is Mom really going to stand by him?

AVERY. Unless it gets too disgusting.

ALMA. It would have to get really disgusting before Mom would let Hillary out-loyalty her. Hillary stood by her man who stuck a cigar in his intern, what could be more disgusting?

AVERY. I don't know, if it turns out he killed her?

ALMA. Do you think he killed her?

AVERY. It doesn't seem like something he would do.

ALMA. He does a lot of things we don't think he would do, apparently. These things may be the center of his life, it turns out. He jumps into mosh pits. He fucks girls my age.

AVERY. Or he doesn't.

ALMA. Or he doesn't. God, it makes me nauseous to think
  about it. Not that he's disgusting-looking or anything.
  But I think about him chasing these little interns
  exactly my age and I see him chasing me. I see him
  coming up to me at a party when his wife isn't around.
  I see him buying me a drink at the Fifth Estate. He's
  at the Kennedy Center, scanning the crowd at inter-
  mission. He spots me, in my jeans and leather jacket,
  sneaking down from the cheap seats. He comes up
  to me and asks how I like it so far. While I'm answer-
  ing he looks at my eyes and notices their color. My
  Dad notices the color of my eyes. My Dad checks out
  my tits. My Dad lets me drive his motorcycle and sits
  behind me so I feel him pressing

  (reacting to **AVERY**'s *reaction)*

  I'M SORRY, I CAN'T MAKE IT GO AWAY. Do you think
  he used a condom? Do you think he still has sex with
  Mom? When he sees her at Thanksgiving? Now they're
  saying he's an undistinguished member of the House.
  I never thought of him as undistinguished. He's always
  working. At least we thought he was working, maybe
  he was hitting on secretaries. I can't see him falling
  for those women, their flibbertigibbet acts. But then,
  how would I know what his type is? I guess most people
  assume their Dad's type is their Mom. That's as far as it
  seems necessary to go. I excuse myself and head down
  the red carpeted staircase to the ladies lounge. I get
  lost and end up in a sort of private lobby where the
  doors to all the boxes are. I notice there are tiny dis-
  creet restrooms here too. I slip into the ladies'. As I'm
  coming out he's there, standing just inside the door.
  He puts his hand on my cheek and guides me back in,
  into one of the stalls, his eye fixed on mine, my head
  shaking. I can't believe I have to think about this. I had
  other plans. No one even knew my Dad was a congressman. No one came up to me and asked are you related

to Dan Ferris, the representative from California? It's not like my name was Gore or Dukakis. Now it's like my name is Lewinsky. Maybe I should get married right away. I want to think about something else. He's got to resign, right? Will someone give him a job? Will his friends still talk to him? Does he have friends, or only mistresses? Does he know people from the mosh pits? Why was he stupid enough to get caught? I always thought he was smarter than that. I thought he was smarter than Bill Clinton.

AVERY. Clinton wanted to get caught.

ALMA. Excuse me? He was so afraid to get caught he couldn't come.

AVERY. He wanted to prove his masculinity. He had the worst of both worlds. Deep down all his Ivy League buddies would always see him as a good old boy from some laughable little state. The people he came from would always see him as a guy who couldn't hunt or fish or bring home dinner on the back of his pickup. He never wanted to be a Rhodes Scholar or a good joketeller at cocktail parties. He's from Arkansas, for God's sake. He wanted to hang out with Don Henley.

ALMA. Dad hung out with Don Henley but it didn't occur to me that he was doing it to get laid.

AVERY. I hate to see him taken down this way. "I'm shocked, shocked to find that you were sleeping with an intern." What do you think interns are there for? You got a couple hundred guys, living in a swamp, going from working breakfasts to committee meetings, flying home to see their wives every other weekend if they're lucky. Enter a couple hundred young women, fresh out of college, with a sincere interest in government, who go all starry-eyed at the lapel mikes and the secret service agents. Some of the members of Congress are pretty dumb, but even they can figure this out. In Washington the number one pickup line is, "Come on, let's get you an I.D."

ALMA. Maybe it was an innocent habit. Maybe they reminded him of me. He was mentoring these interns to make karmic amends for his failed relationship with his own daughter, by getting them I.D.'s, showing them the ways of Washington...

AVERY. Buying them jewelry...

ALMA. Having sex with them in his apartment. Christ on a pop tart.

(pause)

The last time I saw him we met for a quick drink. It seemed so adult. But then families like ours could never see each other at all if it weren't for booze.

(pause)

Even before Dad ruined all our lives.

(pause)

Or before his life was ruined for him by an unfortunate coincidence.

(pause)

Maybe she's hiding. She wants to destroy him. She wants everyone to think he's killed her. She made friends with him and played all innocent and then deliberately vanished. It's a vast right-wing conspiracy. Make it go away. I want to think about my dry cleaning. I want to think about my broken laptop. I want to think about my own fucked-up life. You think he destroyed the body? So they wouldn't find...DNA evidence? Pregnancy evidence? Where do you go in the greater Washington area to incinerate a body? How did he do it, did he wring her neck, did he hit her with something, does he have a gun? Maybe she died in an accident and he freaked out. Like with Mary Jo Kopechne. I guess that wouldn't be much better. A little better. No, much better. She's not dead. She's hiding. She's making this happen. She's a psycho little starfucking freak, like Monica Lewinsky. I'll tear her eyes out. Her parents – did you see them? – want to believe she's their innocent little girl. She was 24! In Washington, D.C.! Working for the Bureau of Prisons! She wanted to be an FBI agent, like DANA SCULLY! We're supposed to care about this twit? The last dedicated public servants in the world are being brought down by spoiled Jewish princesses.

AVERY. Is that fair?

ALMA. There was nothing in her fridge except a peanut butter cup. She was eating out every meal even though she didn't have a paying job.

AVERY. She was 24.

ALMA. I'm 24.

AVERY. And you don't have to work. If you didn't want to.

ALMA. Says who?

AVERY. Well, come on.

ALMA. If I wanted to ask for money all the time. You have a job.

AVERY. If you call it a job. I couldn't afford this place if I depended on what the mayor pays me.

ALMA. Do you have interns at your office?

AVERY. No, the mayor's under a court order.

ALMA. *(a look)*

AVERY. Joke. We don't have interns because when people interested in internships call us, we lose the post-it note.

ALMA. No interns? What do you do for sex?

AVERY. Ha ha.

(small pause)

I hope you're not really asking. I'm ten years older than you, surely we're not going to have this conversation now.

ALMA. You're nine years older than me.

(pensive)

I don't know a thing about you.

(beat)

ALMA. *(cont.)* Or Dad. Or Mom. Have I been uninquisitive? Have I been self-involved?

(beat)

Maybe it runs in the family.

(beat)

How many girls do you think there were?

AVERY. In reality? Maybe three or four.

ALMA. What, are you kidding?

AVERY. Unless he's hushed a lot of people up. Think about it, wouldn't you come forward at this point if you'd had an affair of any kind with him?

ALMA. Sure, if I wanted to see my life get sucked into a media circus. Spend all my time with lawyers, flashbulbs, phone calls.

AVERY. *(on "flashbulbs")* But wouldn't you come forward if you thought he was lying? If you thought he had something to hide?

ALMA. I guess that would depend on whether I had feelings for him.

AVERY. How could you have feelings for a guy who uses women like that?

ALMA. You really haven't ever been in love, have you?

AVERY. I just don't know any women that pathetic.

ALMA. Yes you do.

AVERY. *(realizing who she means)* That is not a nice thing to say about your mother. We should call her. Make sure she's all right.

ALMA. *(in Mom's voice)* Thank you, Avery, everything's fine. I'm a little worried about the garden. There are all these people outside the house, you know.

AVERY. But how are you doing?

ALMA. When you've been in politics as long as your father, situations like this will come up from time to time. All we can do is wait for it to sort itself out.

AVERY. I'm not sure it'll ever get sorted out, Mom.

ALMA. Of course it will.

AVERY. There's a good chance they'll never find her. There are 558 other people they never found, and I imagine they looked a lot harder this time. If they don't find her, or her body, it won't be resolved. We'll never know what happened.

ALMA. We know what didn't happen. We know your father had nothing to do with that young woman's disappearance, because he said so, and he's my husband and your father and we believe him.

AVERY. Where do you think she is?

ALMA. I have no idea.

AVERY. Do you think he was sleeping with her?

ALMA. He said he wasn't.

(*pause*)

AVERY. Actually, he didn't say that.

ALMA. Have you spoken to the mayor about this?

AVERY. Have I – ? He's been out of the office –

ALMA. You need to speak to him. Tell him to tell his Keystone Kops to stop spending so much time on CNN and figure out what happened to that poor girl.

AVERY. I'm not sure he'll listen to me.

ALMA. You speak to him. You call him right now.

AVERY. I can't call him right now, he's –

ALMA. You must have his cell number.

AVERY. I can't call him right now.

ALMA. Avery. I have all these people on the lawn. I wouldn't have thought you'd speak to me that way. Your family needs you. I would have thought you'd be the first one to respond to that.

AVERY. I think I always have.

ALMA. This thing is going to blow over. It's not the first time something like this has happened.

AVERY. I wanted to ask you about that, actually –

ALMA. *(on "about")* But we all have to face that it is a crisis. We need to show a unified front.

AVERY. I feel like I need some more information –

ALMA. This is not a time to be thinking of your needs.

AVERY. I just think some background would help –

ALMA. You need to get on the phone and call in some favors.

AVERY. I don't know if the best thing for me –

ALMA. This is not about you.

AVERY. No, it's about Ilona Waxman. Five feet four inches, brown hair, green eyes, missing for 13 days. Last seen canceling her health club membership. You big jerk.

ALMA. *(in her own voice)* "You big jerk?"

AVERY. You heartless statue – you greeting card – you Stepford Wife –

ALMA. You dumb bimbo.

AVERY. YOU DUMB BIMBO, WHAT THE HELL'S THE MATTER WITH YOU?

ALMA. She was pregnant, you know.

AVERY. Who?

ALMA. Mom. When they got married. She was pregnant with you.

AVERY. I know that. I don't think that means anything.

ALMA. It means they had to get married.

AVERY. It's not that I don't get the point, Alma. I just don't think it means anything.

ALMA. I'm trying to understand the generational thing. I'm trying to find something that humanizes them.

AVERY. We have no proof that Dad is not human. You can't call someone not human just because he marries a robot. That's racist. Even if the robot was pregnant. Wait, does this mean I'm a toaster?

ALMA. He's worse than a robot. He's a politician. His girlfriend is missing and he's worried about getting reelected.

AVERY. He should be worried.

ALMA. He just needs to tell the truth. Isn't that obvious?

AVERY. Depends on what the truth is.

ALMA. Maybe Mom did it. Out of jealousy.

AVERY. And he's taking the fall to protect her. It's a great American love story.

ALMA. Work with me here. A woman may be dead.

AVERY. Yes, but the important thing is how it affects us.

ALMA. You think this is easy for me?

AVERY. Are you kidding? It's like wish fulfillment. If only I could find the documents in the bottom of the sock drawer that prove I was adopted. If only I could find the evidence that proves my parents are murderers. I was right to hate them all along.

(He sips his beer. His customary agitated tempo is starting to slow down.)

Did you ever think maybe he's got a point about not being a perfect man?

ALMA. You're drunk.

AVERY. I live in this town. You don't. Our parents married young, as you so delicately point out. They become pillars of the community. The public servant who seems to know every man in his district by their first name. The guy who seems to have helped every road get fixed, every zoning problem get pushed through. Who in the course of his career has done a favor for four out of five people in Merced County. He smiles, he shakes their hands, he goes to work early and stays late. They send him to Washington. There's all these people to meet. Everybody and his dog wants to take you out to dinner. You're always in restaurants, you're always at receptions, you always have a glass in your hand. Here I am, I'm Dan Ferris. I'm always having my picture taken for this or that thing on the freshman class. The new faces. I find myself seeing my face a lot. I've never been unaware that I'm a fine-looking man.

And when you're in the bar at the InterContinental watching some average-looking assistant chief of staff to the junior senator from Tennessee making time with a beautiful, stylish...you begin to see it as giving in to the inevitable. Unless you're, I don't know, unless you're David Souter.

(**AVERY** *has slipped into DAN's voice.*)

AVERY. *(cont.)* I never wanted to cheat on my wife. But this is Washington, D.C. – and this was Clinton time. You want to know about Clinton time?

Willie Nelson is the only one who calls Clinton "Bubba" to his face. He takes it from Willie because they go waaaay back. God only knows what they used to get up to. When Bill was in his first term as governor of Arkansas. When no one cared. He never worried about what he was doing as governor, because no one in Arkansas cares about fixing things. All Bill thought about was how he looked to Washington. He'd fly to D.C. at the drop of a hat. You mention you might be having a quick breakfast meeting with someone from the DNC and Bill would be on a plane by midnight.

Anyway, this was about the time of the Paula Jones trial, when they were getting ready to depose the President on videotape, before anyone knew that Lucianne Goldberg and Linda Tripp were dropping the dime. There was a thing at the Century Plaza in L.A. for some schmuck's campaign. Willie was there. He was never asked to sing at a fundraiser because of the tax evasion thing, guys were afraid the video would come back to haunt them, but he was there with all those L.A. people, Keith Richards, Tom Jones, you know. Everybody loves Tom Jones. He's a mensch, is what Lou Reed told me. Bill loves to have guys like that come up to his suite afterwards and smoke cigars and play a couple songs. Bill Clinton – here's the thing nobody understands about Bill. He was born with this head for policy, this head for details, he loves that shit, he accepts this is what he's good at. But what he WANTS is to be Lindsey Buckingham.

So Keith is twanging some bluesy notes as we sample cigars. Everybody in the world sends Bill cigars. He travels with a suitcase just for cigars. He's a cigar GEEK. He can tell you the shape of the leaf on this one plant that only grows on Grand Cayman. Details. Keith never actually plays a song – I don't think he likes to expend the energy. He was born to slouch with one leg over the arm of a sofa and twang a little here and there as 4 a.m. becomes 5 a.m.

Now you've got, I'm sorry, but two of the best-looking politicians in America, me and Bill, drinking single malt and smoking cigars. You've got Willie Nelson. You've got Keith Richards. The conversation is not about welfare reform. We're talking about girls. Keith is shooting his mouth off about the women in rock today. Rock used to have real women, he says. Joni. Marianne. Grace Slick. Women with TITS. Now you have these porcupines. Punching holes in their faces. This what's her name, Atlantis Morissette. This Courtney Love, fuck. Courtney Love? Let me tell you: she fucking killed him. I fucking met her.

"Really?" I say. They all look at me. Embarassed. They think I've made a faux pas. The one thing these guys cannot tolerate is if you act like a starstruck little boy. They want to let their hair down and be Guys. They want to order a pizza. I need to clarify what I meant by "Really?" So I say: "I thought Kurt and Courtney were really in love. Like John and Yoko. Everybody may hate Yoko, but nobody questions that they were really in love."

Willie – who's quiet, which is what makes him such a good friend for Bill – Willie pipes up. "I'm still mad at Yoko. I'm sorry, but some things you don't forgive. You know how you drive across the country, you always see pickups with those bumper stickers that say 'Jane

Fonda – unamerican traitor bitch!'? I'm going to get a sticker that says 'Yoko Ono – she broke up the Beatles!'"

Bill downs the end of his drink. That was a bad day, he says. That kid from Nirvana. How old was he? I told Stephanopolous, I want to say something. He goes, "You can't say something. The kid was a known drug addict. Besides, nobody who votes will know what you're talking about." I tell him listen you little creep. Teenagers in every state are hearing this news and thinking, I'm going to do it too, just like he did. He says to me, "Mr. President, I hate to tell you this, but those kids are not going to change their mind because the President of the United States tells them to. They don't look up to you. They looked up to the junkie."

Bill sits there with his cigar brooding about this.

I say, Mr. President, that's wrong. That's wrong. If Tony Bennett died, you'd say something. If YOGI BERRA died, you'd say something. We're talking about a man who saved rock and roll. A man who saved us from listening to Gloria Estefan and Snoop Doggy Dogg the rest of our lives. We're talking about this generation's Keith Richards. This generation's Willie Nelson. I don't care what he did in his private life. Does anyone care about Cole Porter's private life? Does anyone care about Dolly Parton's private life? A great American songwriter is a great American songwriter and his country should honor him. This man changed my life and I'm not ashamed to say so.

There's some pensive puffing as we all reflect on my words. Then Keith mumbles, I thought I was this generation's Keith Richards. More silence. Bill looks a little sleepy. Willie says, "Dan?" "Yes, Willie?" "What are you suggesting about Dolly Parton's personal life?"

ALMA. I thought this was going to be about all the girls everyone nailed.

AVERY. Right. Where was I going with this?

ALMA. When does Ted Kennedy join the party? Ted never wanted to cheat on his wife either. You would not believe the pressure in this town.

AVERY. *(tosses an extra pillow onto the couch)* My head hurts. Do you have all the sheets you need?

ALMA. Don't ask me what happened during the world peace summit when the Dalai Lama was left alone with Mother Teresa and Elie Wiesel.

AVERY. Fine, fine, fine. In early manhood, Dad realized he would always want to be around young women. He made a list of careers that would make this possible – lifeguard, schoolteacher, acting coach, film producer, OB/GYN, carny – and decided that congressman required the least training. Plus you get to be on TV all the time. As a joke, probably, in the late night monologue. Maybe that'll be me someday. That's what public service – and I believe in the concept of public service, because I'm, because I'm an idiot, I guess – it means late nights and breakfast meetings and all you get is complaints. I can see how it happens, when you finally get up from your desk and look out the window at the silence and the Washington monument and the moon, who wouldn't want some comfort, some simple release, I sound like a pig.

ALMA. No.

AVERY. I can see ending up like that. I'll tell you the secret everyone in public service knows, whether they're trying to make a difference in Washington or trying to make a difference in Clayton County, Georgia. And I'm sorry to say this but it's the only thing I've learned: No good deed goes unpunished.

*(**AVERY** starts to go off.)*

ALMA. Wait. Listen.

AVERY. I need ibuprofen.

ALMA. She smashes the plates. He walks out. What if he never sees her again?

AVERY. Oh, Alma.

(AVERY collapses in a chair, giving up. ALMA is more and more animated, with a kind of desperation.)

ALMA. When those plates shatter on the floor it's like an alarm goes off. He wakes up. He realizes, I'm playing with fire. I'm going to ruin my career. And like that, he never sees her again. He never speaks to her again. He won't take her calls. That's why she calls him fifty times on the day she vanishes. Because he won't call her back. She leaves fifty messages for him. He knows that. He knows she's in love with him and it's killing her, she's at the end of her rope, and yet he turns away from her. Because he's afraid, like Clinton, he's afraid. She is utterly bereft. She's convinced herself that they're going to run away together, she's made up this whole movie in her head, she's packing her suitcase to elope with a congressman old enough to be her father. She knows he really loves her. And all the time she calls him.

I know you're there. I know you'll get back to me soon. Dan, please call me and let me know what time is our flight to Cancún. Dan, should I meet you at the airport? Dan, I'm getting worried. Dan, I know I haven't always been there for you but we can work it out. Dan, I'm sorry about the dishes.

Dan. I want you to know that even though you're a selfish, cruel, evil son of a bitch, I loved you more than anyone could ever love you. This is the last message I'm leaving you. By now you're probably just deleting them anyway. In a minute I'm going to take a walk – down to the Potomac. Slip into the water. Swim for a little while – out to the middle of the river. Then just drift. And wait.

(Lights fade.)

NEW YORK CITY

(The voice of a CNN reporter.)

CNN REPORTER. It has been a little over a year since Ilona Waxman was reported missing. Until today, there had been little progress in the case. If you're just joining us, we are still waiting for the medical examiner's report on the manner and cause of death. The police do say that in the last 24 hours they have found quote "quite a bit of the skeletal remains" unquote. The discovery was made by a man searching for turtles in what is described as "a very inaccessible area."

(As the voice continues, the lights come up on a coffee shop. The counter where you order drinks is just offstage. ALMA sits at a table watching the TV, which sits on a high shelf in the corner, facing upstage.)

Family spokeswoman Maureen Brown described Waxman's parents, Sheila and John, and younger brother Seth as "very emotional" after they were informed that an identification had been made.

(AVERY enters carrying a briefcase. He approaches ALMA's table, halts to stare at the TV.)

House staffers said Dan Ferris watched the police announcement on television in a cloakroom in the Capitol. His office later released a statement saying "Congressman Dan Ferris and family want to express their heartfelt sorrow and condolences to the Waxman family." A source close to Ferris said the congressman was "genuinely sad," and that he, like everyone, hoped she would turn up alive. We'll have more from Rock Creek Park in just a moment.

(CNN theme music)

ALMA. Who do you think will play her in the movie?

AVERY. The movie has structural problems. Good beginning. Killer ending. No middle.

ALMA. Thanks for coming.

AVERY. I was coming anyway.

ALMA. To the Waldorf, not to Carmine Street. How was
your flight?

AVERY. I drove. I don't like to fly anymore.

ALMA. Who does?

AVERY. Do you find that you hate to give your name?
When I check in at a hotel or whatever the girl sees
the name Ferris and there's this tiny reaction. Then
I have to wonder if she's going to ask me "Any rela-
tion?" and I'm going to have to decide whether to lie.
Or be, what, sort of defiant. "He's my father." Not that
it comes up because most people don't ask. And when
they do, I always lie. When I'm outside of Washington.
If it's someone unimportant. Like the car rental guy.

(Unnoticed by ALMA *and* AVERY, *a dark-haired woman
enters the coffee shop with the* Times *under her arm,
crosses the stage and goes off to place her order. More
about her later.)*

ALMA. *(watching the TV)* What's going to happen?

AVERY. I guess that depends on the autopsy.

ALMA. What are they going to autopsy?

AVERY. Maybe they'll search the stomachs of the local squir-
rels.

(He reads ALMA*'s look.)*

Sorry.

ALMA. You heard from Dad today?

(She reads AVERY*'s look.)*

Didn't think so.

AVERY. What's he going to say? He's already issued a statement. No point in listening to him issue the same
statement to us.

ALMA. I've got a few statements I'd like to issue to him.

AVERY. It'll be the same as the emails we get from him. "I
just want to thank you kids for standing by me." After a
year of that, he's not going to suddenly open up to us.

ALMA. If he could look into my eyes and say "I did not kill Ilona Waxman," I would feel so much better I would listen to anything he wanted to say.

AVERY. You would not, Alma. You'd turn it on him.

ALMA. *(defensive)* I can hear his side.

AVERY. You're one of the angriest people I know.

ALMA. *(genuinely shocked)* Wow. I. Really?

AVERY. I mean, when it comes to this.

ALMA. No, that's not what you meant.

AVERY. Yes.

ALMA. *(continuous)* You mean I'm angry all the time.

AVERY. I didn't mean it.

ALMA. *(continuous)* That's what you think I am. You think I don't listen, you think I don't care, you think I only want to blame. You sound like my boyfriend.

AVERY. Who's your boyfriend? You have a boyfriend?

ALMA. My ex-boyfriend. I can listen. People open up to me.

AVERY. Good. Who?

ALMA. *(gathering her things)* Well, it was good to catch up. You must have things to do at the Waldorf. Put your shirts in the drawer. Alphabetize the minibar.

AVERY. Look, I'm sorry.

ALMA. Jesus, Avery.

AVERY. I'm sorry. Sit down. Let's call him.

ALMA. Right now?

AVERY. He could really be in trouble.

ALMA. He hasn't called us.

AVERY. He's not going to call us, we have to call him.

(**ALMA** *still hasn't sat down.* **AVERY** *has his phone out.*)

ALMA. Put that away.

AVERY. Come on, we'll practice. I'll be Dad.

ALMA. You always get to be Dad. I always have to be the angry chick.

AVERY. I said I didn't mean it.

ALMA. The angriest chick you've ever met in your life.

AVERY. I'll be the angry chick. I mean, I'll be you. I'll be you and you be Dad. Okay? I dial. Dad's cellphone rings. He checks the screen. It says "Alma."

ALMA. *(caught up in it)* Does he answer?

(**AVERY** *makes ringing sound.* **ALMA** *"answers."*)

ALMA. *(as Dan)* Hello? Alma?

AVERY. Dad.

ALMA. How are you?

AVERY. How are you?

ALMA. You must be watching the news.

AVERY. Yeah. I wanted to ask you… are you surprised they found the body?

ALMA. Yes, I'm surprised. I thought I would see her again. I don't think I completely gave up hope. I thought my phone might ring and I'd hear her voice, saying it was all a joke, I was just mad at you.

AVERY. Aren't you being an awfully sweet Dad?

ALMA. Shut up, don't break character. I hate to think of her lying there, wasting away, being – devoured. You can't imagine, seeing it on TV, someone you loved – standing in the House cloakroom – the other guys watching too but keeping their distance from me in little clumps. Does anyone put a hand on my shoulder? As they show that helicopter shot of the park and I have to listen to them tell the story of the big bad wolf, the sleazy lying politician who ate up the little girl on her way to grandmother's house. What gives them the right to talk about us that way? Do you know what it's like to fall in love with someone and know that it's impossible because you're at different points in your life?

(*During the following, the woman re-enters with a giant mug of coffee and sits at an empty table with her newspaper. She is 28 and looks exactly like* **MONICA LEWINSKY**. **AVERY** *and* **ALMA** *don't notice her.*)

AVERY. Different points like you're a married womanizer congressman and she's 24? That's not impossible, that's typical.

ALMA. Yes, it's typical, but what if this is different? I wasn't in control. I had to see her. After twenty years of cautious undetected affairs I couldn't use my head because there was something about her. That acid streak she had, the way she had no illusions about Washington... The way she pressed her cheek against my chest when we slept... the way she looked at me like I was everything she wanted...

AVERY. The way she showed up anywhere you told her to and slept with you and left and never complained...

ALMA. I'm trying to tell you I miss her.

AVERY. *(overlapping)* Or was it her gym-toned body?

ALMA. *(overlapping)* I wish I could hold her again.

AVERY. *(overlapping)* Or was it her tits?

ALMA. Don't talk about her that way! I get this from the whole world, do I have to listen to it from you?

AVERY. You have no rights in this situation. You're a terrible rotten person who lies to everyone.

ALMA. I never lied to you. I never lied to Ilona.

AVERY. You did lie to Ilona. Didn't you tell her – didn't you tell all your mistresses that your wife was an invalid?

(beat)

ALMA. Not in so many words.

AVERY. Finally, we arrive in Clintonland! I'm disappointed.

ALMA. One lie. A lie which contained the truth that I was lonely. I never said your mother was on her deathbed. I never said I would divorce her. I never gave Ilona false expectations. I treated her like an adult.

AVERY. Was that a favor?

ALMA. I didn't treat her like Bill treated Monica. I didn't treat her like a whore.

MONICA. Giving blowjobs makes you a whore?

(**ALMA** *and* **AVERY** *turn from their heated argument to realize that* **MONICA** *has been watching them. They are speechless.*)

MONICA. *(cont.)* Are you doing this for an acting class? My manager wanted me to take an acting class but I was pretty sure being around that many people would make me throw up.

AVERY. It's a game.

MONICA. Oh. Fun.

(In the ensuing deathly pause, the three become aware of an interview being shown on the TV and turn to watch.) [See appendix for additional TV dialogue.]

LAWYER. *(on TV)* Naturally the Waxmans are in, well, I would describe them as being in a fragile emotional state. Of course, as the months went by, they knew their chances of finding their daughter alive were increasingly remote. But like any parents would have to, I would say they retained some hope right up until receiving Wednesday's phone call about the dental records.

MONICA. They don't usually have the TV on in here. I stopped watching TV. For years. So – in your game – you're Dan Ferris and you're – ? I didn't get who you are.

AVERY. I'm his daughter. That is – um, yeah.

MONICA. That's right. He has a daughter who's like twenty –

ALMA. 25. What do you think happened?

MONICA. I don't know Dan Ferris.

ALMA. But you know something about this kind of thing.

MONICA. Yeah, I know something about this kind of thing.

ALMA. What's it like? Do you think, Look at him. He's got power. He's got it all. He could have anyone he wants. I bet I can make him choose me.

MONICA. No, dummy, you think, that guy is hot. I want to go to bed with him. It's called falling in love. There are songs about it. I'll make you a tape.

AVERY. We try to figure out what it was like. What their relationship was like. What they talked about. What they might have talked about the last time they saw each other.

ALMA. Why don't you be Ilona?

MONICA. Me?

AVERY. Alma, this is embarrassing.

ALMA. Shut up. Avery will be Dan and you be Ilona. It's perfect casting.

MONICA. But I'm not dead.

(pause)

Instead I'm famous. The E! Channel said I was the most famous American woman in the world. More people had heard of me than Madonna. Ilona Waxman had to die to get famous.

ALMA. Did you ever think you were in danger? That you might be killed?

MONICA. I definitely thought I might go to jail. They made that very clear. I thought about jail a lot. Heidi Fleiss went to jail, you know. Of course, she was a professional criminal. I was just a dumb intern.

ALMA. Yeah.

(awkward pause)

MONICA. He told lies about me. He had his people spread the rumor that I was crazy. He broke my heart, tough shit, but to say that about me, it's cowardly. He's not a brave man, William Jefferson Clinton. Afraid of a girl. And it didn't work, either. All it did was hurt me a little more. I went through hell and he's never said a word to me about it. He'll never speak to me again, not till the day he dies. To him I'm a… I'm an error of judgment.

Yeah, I can imagine him thinking about it. Getting me out of the way. I imagine Dan Ferris killing Ilona Waxman. Calling her and saying, meet me in the park at midnight. I find it easy to imagine.

The one thing I find impossible to imagine is ever falling in love again. How would I start dating? "Hi, I'm Monica." You know what I do all day? I practice looking people in the eye.

That's why talking about it or not talking about it is like lose-lose. Either way, I'm the girl on her knees in front of the President. Nobody ever makes jokes about the things HE did to ME. The first time we were together he made me come four times. But you know that: it's in the Starr report. And really, it's about time we used government funding to study the female orgasm.

It's not like I'm the only girl who ever wanted him. I've been reading about JFK. His relationships make our relationship look like, I don't know, I mean we had SOMETHING, we gave each other BOOKS.

You know what's the only pathetic thing about me? It's not pathetic to have a crush on an older married guy who happens to be the most powerful man in the world and radiates enough charisma to set off a Geiger counter. That's foolish, but not pathetic. What's pathetic is having Linda Tripp as a friend. Can you imagine what a fucked-up girl I must be to allow Linda Tripp to become someone I called when I was upset? Someone should do a study on the attraction of the zaftig to the zaftig in the case of Lewinsky, Goldberg and Tripp. There's a law firm. We could specialize in women's issues. Like betrayal.

I remember the first time I called him and he didn't answer. It was after he got freaked out and said we can have no physical contact ever again. I knew he was there, because there was a long series of rings, then that little pause and little click and then a new ring, I mean it was the same ring but it like skipped a beat. I knew he saw my name and he let it go to voicemail. I explained it to myself. He's in an important meeting. He's having a photo taken. Hillary's there. But something had dropped into the bottom of my stomach and it sat there from then on going, "Monica, you know he saw your name and thought 'Oh Jesus, I don't need this today.'"

For a while that was my whole life, that ring. But I kept calling, because whenever he did answer, I forgot how mad I was. We had the best phone sex those months. I've got the President of the United States sitting in the Oval Office holding his cock. That is hot.

That was the year of him getting me fired and then not finding me a job. After he cut it off for whatever it was, the fourth time, the fifth time. Then I was subpoenaed and he invited me to the Christmas party.

I checked my coat and I thought I caught her giving me like, a look. I accepted an eggnog off a tray and I thought I saw him giving me a look, you know? There were all the people I used to work with, were they giving me, were they like whispering behind their glass of champagne to the person next to them? I was sailing through this sea of people and they were parting for me with these looks, these whispers. I was the camera moving through the crowd, from the point of view of the celebrity. She's the one. Knowing they shouldn't stare but staring. And I realized, my whole life has led up to this. I was always meant to be this woman in this room. Soon I will arrive at the far end of the room. I will turn, elegantly, to face them, and say, Thank you all for making me feel so welcome. Yes, I am the president's lover.

But instead I got to the end of the room and there was Doug and he goes "He'll meet you in the Oval Office." He had even more gifts for me than usual, but I had to ask him to give me a Christmas kiss. That's the way I think of him now. That Christmas. He's looking at me and he's Billing me, I know he's Billing me, he's giving me full-on, weapons-grade Bill.

Except, sometimes, when I see a particularly good picture of him, I remember another night. A night he

was working late. Just in front of the Oval Office bathroom there's a spot where you're not picked up by the
security cameras. Most times we were there, but sometimes we were in the bathroom, which is nice, you
know, antique-y. One night he showed me behind the
marble statue thing there's another door. He takes my
hand. We go through the door where the walls are one
foot thick. I go, is this a panic room? Is this an under-
ground fortress? He holds my hand tighter and we go
down this passageway with violet energy-saving lights
in industrial caged brackets on the walls. He stops and
slides open a panel and tells me to look through. It's
a one-way mirror. I'm looking at a conference room.
Sidney and Bob are in there and some other senior
staff with their manila folders and their laptops and
their accordion files.

(whispering)

"It's the Mexico meeting," he's whispering in my ear.
Bob is yelling at someone. I can almost hear him
through the glass.

(whispering)

"I have to call the President of Mexico tomorrow. Do
you want to listen? Do you want to be there when I
call?" His smell is all around me. It's not what he says,
it's the there-ness of him. He's too big to get your mind
around, like the United States of America. He moves
away again, his hand drops to my hand, he takes me
farther along the passage, to where it's darkest. He
presses me against the wall. He opens another panel
just in front of my eyes. The Oval Office. His desk, his
chair, that rug.

(whispering)

"That's where the President sits. In a few hours he'll
pick up one of those phones and talk to the President
of Mexico about the peso. Calls will come in about
forest fires and interest rates. He'll ask his staff on
some things and ignore them on others. He'll drink

coffee out of that mug and talk to them." I turned around and slid down his body. He was hard. His hands were in my hair. It was what I wanted to do for him. I knew he was seeing that empty chair, that empty office, and what the President did there, how few men know what it's like. I tasted him getting ready to come but he wouldn't let me again, he put himself away and I wrapped my arms around him and cried into his chest. It isn't right. It's what I want. I looked up into his eyes but he wasn't looking at me. He was looking at the empty chair.

(**MONICA** *leaves the coffee shop. Silence.*)

AVERY. Where were we?

ALMA. Can we leave?

AVERY. Yeah. I have my car.

ALMA. OK.

(*Lights out on the coffee shop. Tape in.*)

ALMA. (*on TAPE*) We have just a few minutes left. Uh, what effect has this had on your family?

AVERY. (*on TAPE*) Well, it's been tough, I mean, it's been tough on my family. I mean, as I mentioned, uh… they dragged my wife across the country for an interview, because they refused to do it here, and they were going to subpoena her. They tried to uh, go through her medical records, uh, they reported she didn't have thumbs, and they chased my children around. The tabloids have. But the fact of the matter is, this is not about the Ferrises. This is about the Waxmans.

ALMA. (*on TAPE*) Do you fear that uh, the public out there um, may be very disappointed that you didn't come forward and reveal details today, as we sit here tonight?

AVERY. (*on TAPE*) Well, I think I have revealed details.

ALMA. (*on TAPE*) You don't think you're stonewalling.

AVERY. (*on TAPE*) No, I don't think I'm stonewalling at all. I think that people expect that you can maintain some of your privacy. I think the Waxmans expect to maintain some of their daughter's privacy. And I'm trying to honor that. I'm trying to do that with dignity. I, I'm trying to retain some privacy for my family and for their family. And I think your jurors out there will understand that.

(Tape out. Lights fade up on **AVERY** *and* **ALMA** *in the car. It must be clear that they are really in a car, not pretending to be in a car.* **AVERY** *driving. Night has fallen.)*

ALMA. Dan.

AVERY. *(quietly)* I don't want to –

ALMA. Dan.

AVERY. I don't want to.

(pause)

ALMA. Dan.

*(**AVERY** glances at her.)*

I'm not going to tell your wife. I'm not going to write a book. I'm not going to go on *20/20*. I'm going to sit quietly in my apartment on the Lower East Side and wait for the baby to be born. I know you can't change your life overnight. I can wait. I've got six months.

AVERY. *(flatly)* Six.

ALMA. I didn't mean for it to happen, believe me.

AVERY. Oh?

ALMA. Of course not.

(pause)

Maybe you should take me home.

AVERY. I thought you wanted to fuck.

ALMA. Maybe we need some time alone. I mean apart alone.

*(**AVERY** is silent.)*

ALMA. *(cont.)* I don't want you to be unhappy about this. I've made my decision, but a lot of different things can happen now.

(**AVERY** *is silent.*)

Maybe it's best that I move away. Give us some space. Maybe this baby is something I should do by myself. Why don't we agree to talk again after the baby is born?

(**AVERY** *is silent.*)

I'm not going to drag you into something you're not comfortable with. Nobody needs to know.

(**AVERY** *is silent.*)

I'm not going to tell anyone. That's what I've decided. It'll just be me and my baby. It's nobody's business.

(**AVERY** *is silent.*)

I'm sorry I burdened you with this. I shouldn't have told you. Just forget about me, OK? You can forget about me, and I'll forget about you.

(**AVERY** *is silent.*)

Who knocked me up? I don't even remember. There are 435 members of the House.

(**AVERY** *is silent.*)

That's a joke.

(**AVERY** *is silent.*)

I'm sorry I let things get out of hand. It was my fault. I'll take care of it.

(**AVERY** *is silent.*)

Dan? I'm sorry.

(**AVERY** *is silent.*)

Where are we? I really should go home. I don't feel well.

(**AVERY** *is silent.*)

Dan, I'm serious. My stomach has been bad lately.

(**AVERY** *is silent.*)

ALMA. *(cont.)* That's M Street. That's M Street. I can walk from here. You know what? Let me out.

(**AVERY** *is silent.*)

Stop the car, OK?

(**AVERY** *is silent.*)

Dan, I want you to listen to me. I would never do any-thing to hurt you.

(**AVERY** *is silent. Sharp sound of car doors auto-locking. The car speeds up. The lights fade very slowly.*)

End of Play

APPENDIX

Additional TV dialogue for the deathly pause in the coffeehouse scene.

ANCHOR. *(ON TV)*

(This speech can be used underneath the preceding dialogue, and is provided here as a lead-in to the LAWYER's speech.)

What you're seeing here is a live helicopter view of Rock Creek Park, which has been closed off by police. It's been almost 24 hours since the remains found in the park were positively identified by the M.P.D.C. as being the body of Ilona Waxman. Earlier today, we spoke to Paul Shugarman, attorney for the Waxman family, about the family's reaction.

LAWYER. *(ON TV)*

(This speech is heard in the deathly silence following **MONICA**'s *line "Oh. Fun.")*

Naturally the Waxmans are in, well, I would describe them as being in a fragile emotional state. Of course, as the months went by, they knew their chances of finding their daughter alive were increasingly remote. But like any parents would have to, I would say they retained some hope right up until receiving Wednesday's phone call about the dental records.

ANCHOR. *(ON TV)*

(Used as lead-out as the TV volume fades again.)

We turn now to Dr. Nathan Barrett of Atlanta University Medical School to tell us how dental records can provide information in a case like this. Dr. Barrett, thank you for joining us.

OTHER TITLES AVAILABLE FROM SAMUEL FRENCH

MILLICENT SCOWLWORTHY

Rob Handel

Drama / 7m, 5f

A girl found murdered in the cellar on Christmas morning. A massacre at the high school. The grownups of the community want to forget, but the children have begun to meet in the middle of the night to remember. Nine teenagers gather at an overgrown memorial and reenact the story.

OTHER TITLES AVAILABLE FROM SAMUEL FRENCH

CORNELIA

Mark V. Olsen

2m, 3f / Dramatic Comedy

From the co-creator of the hit HBO series '*Big Love*' comes an epic slice of history centering on 1970s Alabama politics. Beautiful, divorced beauty queen Cornelia Folsom is a force of nature who works her way into the heart of Governor George Wallace. Together they plan to take over the state and then the White House until an assassination attempt halts his presidential campaign. But no obstacle is too great for Cornelia to overcome, as she secretly harbors her own political ambitions amidst a hostile campaign staff, her rarely sober mother, and Southern shenanigans in this sweeping, provocative tale of sex, power, and bare-knuckled American politics